The Car Trip

For Jan

PUFFIN PIED PIPER BOOKS
Published by the Penguin Group
Penguin Books USA Inc., 375 Hudson Street, New York, New York 10014, U.S.A.
Penguin Books Ltd, 27 Wrights Lane, London W8 5TZ, England
Penguin Books Australia Ltd, Ringwood, Victoria, Australia
Penguin Books Canada Ltd, 10 Alcorn Avenue, Toronto, Ontario, Canada M4V 3B2
Penguin Books (N.Z.) Ltd, 182-190 Wairau Road, Auckland 10, New Zealand
Penguin Books Ltd, Registered Offices: Harmondsworth, Middlesex, England

First published in hardcover in the United States 1983 by
Dial Books for Young Readers
A Division of Penguin Books USA Inc.

Published in Great Britain by Walker Books Ltd.
Copyright © 1983 by Helen Oxenbury
All rights reserved
Library of Congress Catalog Card Number: 83-5255
Printed in Hong Kong
First Puffin Pied Piper Printing 1994
ISBN 0-14-050377-3
A Pied Piper Book is a registered trademark of
Dial Books for Young Readers, A Division of Penguin Books USA Inc.,
® TM 1,163,686 and ® TM 1,054,312.
1 3 5 7 9 10 8 6 4 2

The Car Trip

by Helen Oxenbury

A Puffin Pied Piper

One day we went for a ride.
We took along some sandwiches.

I made believe I was a lion.
"How can Daddy drive properly
with all that noise?" Mommy said.

I went with Daddy to pay for the gas.
"Can I please have some candy?" I said.

At lunchtime we went to a cafeteria.
I only wanted ice cream.

"Take a nap now," Mommy said.
"We won't be home till late."
"I have to go to the bathroom," I said.

"I think it's going to rain,"
 Mommy said.
"I feel sick," I said.
"Quick! Stop!" Mommy shouted.

We cleaned up the car.
Then it wouldn't start again.
Daddy tried and tried,
but nothing happened.
"Call a garage for help!" he said.

A truck towed us home.
I got to sit next to the driver.
"Today was the best car trip ever!"
I told my friends.

About the Author/Artist

Helen Oxenbury is internationally recognized as one of the finest children's book illustrators, with over thirty books to her credit, including *We're Going on a Bear Hunt* and *The Dragon of an Ordinary Family* (Dial) by Margaret Mahy. Her Very First Books®—five board books for toddlers—have been newly designed and reissued by Dial. According to *The Washington Post*, the books "will delight parents and entertain infants." *The Bulletin of the Center for Children's Books* applauded, "Fun, but more than that: These are geared to the toddler's interests and experiences." Ms. Oxenbury lives in London.